Diary of an ACCIDENTAL WiTCH

HALLOWEEN BALL

W0007124

TO LITTLE WITCHES EVERYWHERE, THIS ONE
IS FOR YOU, H AND P XX

FOR ARCHIE AND OLIVE, MY LOCKDOWN
HEROES, LOVE MUM X

tiger tales

5 River Road, Suite 128, Wilton, CT 06897
Published in the United States 2023
Originally published in Great Britain 2021
by Little Tiger Press Ltd.
Text copyright © 2021 Perdita & Honor Cargill
Illustrations copyright © 2021 Katie Saunders
ISBN-13: 978-1-6643-4058-9
ISBN-10: 1-6643-4058-0
Printed in China
STP/3800/0508/0123
2 4 6 8 10 9 7 5 3 1

www.tigertalesbooks.com

Diary of an ACCIDENTAL WITCH

HALLOWEEN BALL

BY PERDITA & HONOR CARGILL

ILLUSTRATED BY KATIE SAUNDERS

tiger tales

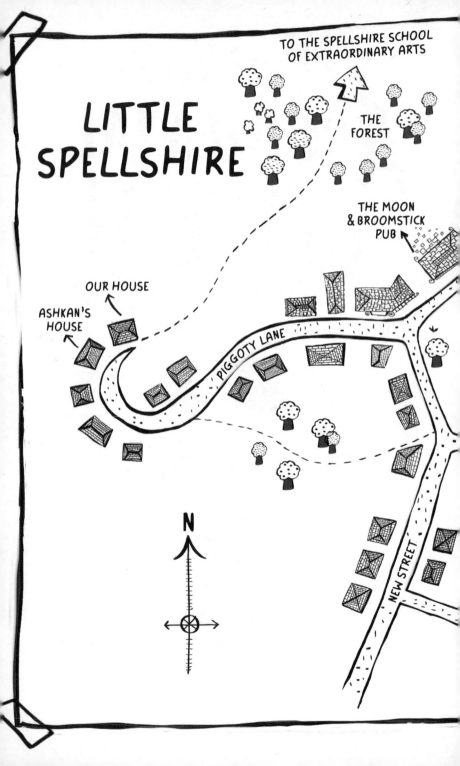

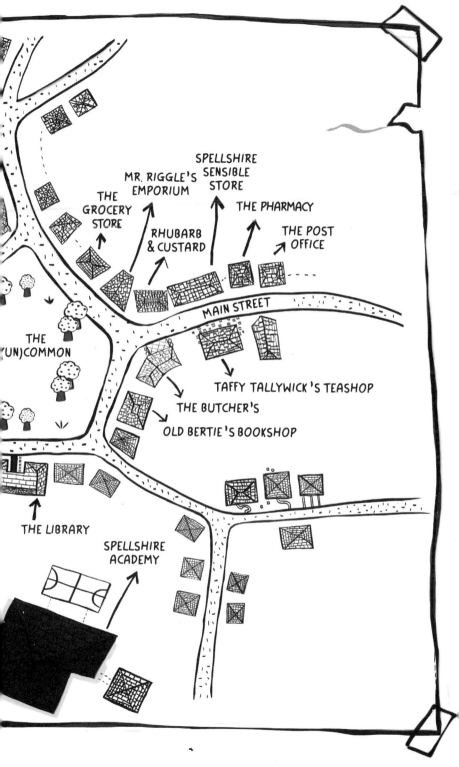

PRIVATE
TOP SECRET

PROPERTY OF
BEA BLACK

ABOUT ME!

- **Name:** Bea Black
- **Age:** 11 _→ for 3 whole weeks now!_
- **Address:** Little Spellshire*, Spellshire
- **Lives with:** DADI Ben Black (weather scientist writing a book about the very peculiar weather in Little Spellshire). Also STAN the class frog.

- **Goes to school at:** Little Spellshire's School of Extraordinary Arts** (but only because Dad made a terrible mistake)
- **Best friend:** Ashkan (Ash) Namdar - lives next door and goes to the Academy (the ORDINARY non-witch school).
- **Favorite food:** Toast and fluffmallows***

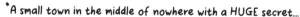

*A small town in the middle of nowhere with a HUGE secret....
**V. V. secret WITCH SCHOOL!!!!!
***The sweetest, FLUFFIEST snack known to witches.

HOPES & DREAMS:

- Change schools to go to the **Academy** (preferably before HALLOWEEN) so I can be with Ash and not have to worry about things like LEVITATION ever again!!
- Make more friends in Little Spellshire.
- Get a puppy.

CHALLENGES & WORRIES:

- SURVIVE being at witch school! Obviously. (This will be extreeeeemely difficult because I can't use a wand or do any spells or potions and everyone says I'm a **TOADBRAIN**.)
- So many worries!!! (For example keeping secrets, making friends, and finding a missing miniature pig....)
- Currently no. 1 worry: My potions homework. I'm supposed to go to Nightshade Glade in the deep, dark forest in the middle of the night to find ingredients to brew a magic potion.... HELP!!

11:02 a.m. School

Dad finally sent the application for me to move to the **Academy**, where there are no witches AT ALL. But for now, I'm stuck at Extraordinary, it's only break time, and I've already had to retreat to my favorite broom cupboard with Stan the class frog for a little rest.

I don't think anyone—except maybe Winnie—likes starting Monday with double physics (aka wand work), but it's extra hard if you can't make anything go up in the air. And now I'm panicking about potions. Even if the **Academy** replies at broomstick speed, it's probably not going to be fast enough to get me out of doing my Frost Moon homework!

1:55 p.m.

Have just spent forever searching for Professor Agu's miniature pig, Excalibur, but nobody has seen him since he went flying out the classroom window last Thursday.

Fabi says he's probably having a wonderful time in the Deep, Dark Forest, but now I'm very worried about WEREWOLVES and it's all my fault! Pretty sure I wouldn't have to worry about this kind of thing at the Academy.

The Extraordinary: Halloween Issue 1

Sports News and Notices

- Congratulations to the ninth grade Shooting Stars who <u>crushed</u> the grade ten Flying Cauldrons by 231 goals to 165.

- Ms. Celery would like to remind all GOers that head-on broom-bumping is an ILLEGAL MOVE that (if seen) will be penalized. We all wish Gerty Twistle a speedy recovery.

Halloween Ball Notices

- Sixth and seventh grade: Applications to join the Junior Halloween Ball Committee (with particular responsibility for menu choices and decoration) must be made to Ms. Sparks <u>no later than 4:30 p.m. Friday</u>.

- Grades eight, nine, and ten: Those who wish to join the teachers on the Senior Halloween Ball Committee are very welcome. Planning meetings will be Wednesday and Friday after school in the Little Library. Just show up with your BEST ideas!

Quick-fire Q & A with Ms. Sparks!

Q: Favorite time of the year?

A: Halloween of course!

Q: Favorite pet?

A: *Long pause while principcal thinks* ~~Um, I had a dog when I was little, a cockerpoo named Bubble~~ ZEPHYR OF COURSE!

Q: Favorite joke?

A: What goes cackle, cackle, bonk? A witch laughing her head off!

Thank you, Ms. Sparks!

Dear Agony Witch

Dear Agony Witch,

X in my class is a twin. Y in my class is also a twin. X and Y keep swapping places and then laughing at me when I call them by the wrong name. While the rest of the class finds this very funny, I feel it is undermining my authority. I cannot tell which witch is which. What should I do?

Yours,

A Worried Teacher

Dear Worried Teacher,

I suggest you turn one into a warthog, easily distinguished from a witch. Problem solved. Have a great year.

Love,

Agony Witch x

3:25 p.m. School

"I hope you're all doing well with the preparations for that potion I set you last week," says Miss Lupo, demonstrating the best way to use a pestle and mortar. "Get busy collecting your tears of a baboon, cuckoo flowers, and poor man's treacle, and don't forget that the night of the full Frost Moon is an excellent one for magical concoctions."

And the best night of the year to dig for skeledrake roots!

I catch Blair's eye and smile shyly. She might not have been the most welcoming witch in the class when I came to Extraordinary, and she doesn't give off a very friendly vibe, but if she hadn't given me those extra notes when I missed class, I'd never had known that I had to go to Nightshade Glade at midnight and dig for skeledrakes while performing a SONG AND DANCE routine for the lunar spirits!

3:29 p.m.
Worrying a little because I'm even worse at singing and dancing than I am at potions. Must figure out how to get to Nightshade Glade.

Blair's notes

POTIONS NOTES

The most potent ingredient in this potion is the fingerlength of skeledrake root, which will be added, under supervision, to the other prepared ingredients in class. Bulbs grow five inches deep under the knotted roots of the great elm in Nightshade Glade and MUST be extracted following these instructions:

* Leave your house no earlier than eleven o'clock, nor later than quarter past on the night of the full Frost Moon.
* Take with you a small iron digging implement and a creature, <u>strong in fang</u>, to help you drag the root from the garound.
* POLITELY direct your broomstick to take you to Nightshade Glade, taking the as-the-crow-flies route.
* When you reach Nightshade Glade, first honor the spirit of the Frost Moon by singing an original song and then the spirits of the forest by performing an original dance.
* On the <u>stroke of midnight</u>, dig for the roots, and when you have found them, call upon your creature to drag them from their hiding place.

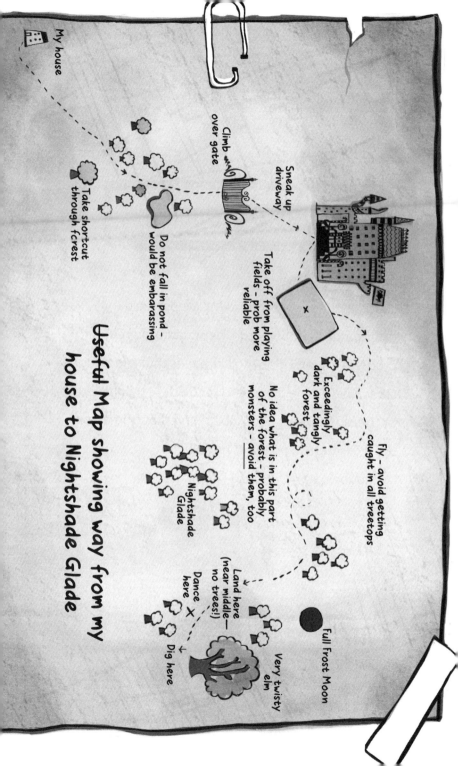

Useful Map showing way from my house to Nightshade Glade

My house

Take shortcut through forest

Climb over gate

Sneak up driveway

Do not fall in pond - would be embarrassing

Take off from playing fields - prob more reliable

Exceedingly dark and tangly forest

No idea what is in this part of the forest - probably monsters - avoid them, too

Fly - avoid getting caught in all treetops

Nightshade Glade

Land here (near middle— no trees!)

Full Frost Moon

Very twisty elm

Dance here X

Dig here

WEDNESDAY OCTOBER 6

3:45 p.m. School

Just got out of physics and Mr. Muddy said my attempt at levitating Stan "demonstrated real progress." What I didn't tell him was that that was *at least* ninety-nine percent* due to Stan's helpful leap at the big moment. "You'll be flying that frog across the classroom in no time," he said.

Maybe not.

*One hundred percent!

THURSDAY OCTOBER 7

10:55 a.m. School

BEST news. Ms. Celery flew into the middle of our zoology class, looking hot and very upset. Well, that wasn't the best news—the *best* news was that Excalibur has turned up alive and well in her gym bag.

I'm not a miniature-pig murderer!

I'm lucky she found him because that bag is SO big and SO full of peculiar things that he could have been in there for days with nothing to eat but energy bars and nothing to drink but get-better potions.

Professor Agu was so happy he forgot all about testing us on the magical properties of ducks and let us out early for the break.

Ms Celery's gym bag contents:

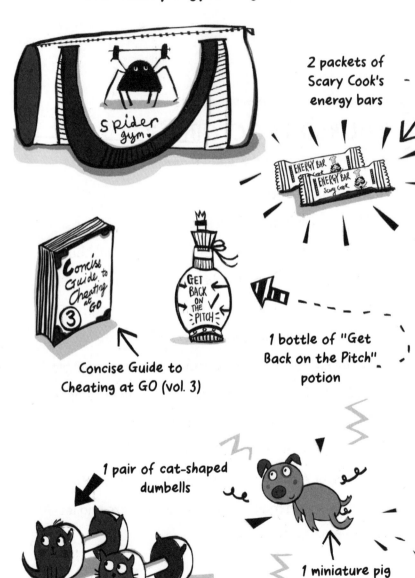

2 packets of Scary Cook's energy bars

Concise Guide to Cheating at GO (vol. 3)

1 bottle of "Get Back on the Pitch" potion

1 pair of cat-shaped dumbells

1 miniature pig

FRIDAY OCTOBER 8
(FROST MOON EVE! EEEEEEK!!!)

11:01 a.m. School

| DODOS: 52 | DRAGONS: 40 |

I'm getting good at this broomstick-flying GO game! Ms. Celery asked me to be co-captain of the Dodos after the holiday break! I was so excited I forgot to tell her I'd probably have moved schools by then.

12:15 p.m.

It is a shame that PE is followed by math.

Mr. Smith kept me after class for a Little Chat. "Do you have any idea what could happen if you get the math in a potion wrong?" he asked kindly

before embarking on a terrifying story about a student who magicked a mouse the size of a rhino. "You can crack this, Bea Black," he said as I was finally escaping. "And, if you get stuck again, just come and ask me and I'll help you."

I like Mr. Smith now. Still don't like fractions, though.

2:47 p.m.

Very useful Friday lecture about trees. I'm now ~~a bit~~ confident that I will be able to recognize an ELM.

Then the tenth graders did an aerial acrobatics display that as far as I could tell had absolutely nothing to do with trees, but it was so *amaaaazzzzinggg*

I clapped until my hands hurt. (Maybe if I was invisible, and *nobody ever asked me to do MAGIC,*[*] this school would be okay???)

3:35 p.m.

Things are looking up on the Potions front! Amara asked me if I wanted her spare cuckoo flowers, but before I could thank her, much less ask if she had any helpful tips on skeledrakes, she shoved a brown paper bag of the flowers into my hand and flew off. Oh, well, I guess I'll see her in the forest tomorrow night and can thank her then.

5:21 p.m. Home

Mrs. Slater on reception had seemed surprised when, instead of checking Stan into his cubbyhole at dismissal time, I asked to keep him for the weekend. At first, I thought she was going to say no, but it was just her very-angry-tortoise face.

"What do you want with *him*?" she asked, looking

[*] Or original song-and-dance routines.

at Stan as though he were a very disappointing frog. Excuse me! Stan is, in his own way, a FABULOUS frog. But that wasn't why I was taking him on a little vacation to 1 Piggoty Lane. I still need a creature strong in fang, and even if Stan's teeth are tiny, any toothed creature has to be better than none. Probably.

"You can dig up a skeledrake root—whatever that is—can't you?" I'd asked him while we were walking home (well, I was walking; Stan was in my cape pocket). He hadn't given me what you could call a direct answer, but when I peeked at him, he didn't look any more downbeat than usual, so I was taking that as a YES.

5:52 p.m.

"You don't happen to know what poor man's treacle is, do you?" I asked Dad, on the off-chance.

"Garlic," he replied without missing a beat. "Haven't heard it called that in a long time." My dad is literally a GENIUS. "Why do you want to know?"

"School quiz on old plant names," I ~~lied~~ said, and he nodded happily, like that made perfect sense. He doesn't seem to mind that there's a frog on the kitchen table—completely bought my garbled ~~second lie~~ explanation about Observing Wild Creatures Up Close for zoology. In fact, he was so impressed by the enlightened teaching methods *blah blah* at Extraordinary that it might have hurt my Move School Campaign.

Tragically, he's never heard of baboon tears, so I think I'll just substitute my own and hope for the best. I've checked off *almost* everything on page two of my potions homework!

Honestly, if it wasn't for the whole skeledrakes-midnight-digging thing, I'd be chill about this homework.

6:33 p.m.

I've discovered Stan likes ~~burned~~ crispy fish sticks! I'm not sure that's okay. It's practically CANNIBALISM. For a small frog he has a big appetite.

8:13 p.m.

Ash came over—he just left.

"Is that a FROG on your head?" he asked the minute he came through the door.

"Of course," I said, nodding (*carefully*). Then I remembered this wasn't NORMAL and blabbered out my zoology excuse. Ash looked confused. Apparently, the only frogs that turn up in lessons at the **Academy** have been dead for some time. He started to tell me about a "fun" dissection class, but it was too scary for Stan* so I had to make him stop. Then he asked me if I wanted to go over to his house tomorrow—some of his friends from school were coming over to watch soccer and eat pizza. For about two seconds, I was really happy and then I remembered....

Nooooo!

My first invitation to a sort-of-party in Little Spellshire and I can't go because I'll be too BUSY preparing to FLY off into the forest to DIG and perform a midnight SONG-AND-DANCE routine.

I am NOT really happy anymore.

*Look, I can't be SURE he understands, but I can't be sure he doesn't!!!!

I said I'd be finishing my homework and Ash looked at me like I was a tragic *worm* and went home in a huff.

9:13 p.m.

Turns out a) crying on command is very hard (even after my big disappointment about missing out on pizza and soccer) and b) collecting tears in an old shampoo bottle is even harder. I might just use water with a little salt—it's all the same, isn't it?

9:32 p.m.

Dad heard me "crying" and came up to ask me if I had *friend problems*.

I said NO quite aggressively because of not having very many friends at all, and then we (Stan, too) sat on the edge of my bed in silence for five minutes.

"Well, something's wrong," Dad said at last.

"How did you know?" I asked, which was very SILLY and he said that even if I hadn't been "howling like a sad dog" it was "written all over my face."

For a minute, I let myself imagine what it would
be like to tell Dad what was going on, because even
though he probably wouldn't have any tips on digging
up skeledrakes, he'd make me feel better. Instead,
I asked him if he'd managed to find out if I could
transfer schools and he said that he hadn't wanted to
mention it earlier when I sounded so upbeat about my
homework (!) but actually YES, the request has been
submitted. Then he looked at me sadly, handed me a
tissue, and said it was likely for the best because he
wasn't *convinced* I'd settled in at Extraordinary.

So ... that's good news.

"Of course," he said, handing me the whole box of
tissues, "there's no guarantee that the Academy
will agree to take you."

Might manage to collect those tears after all.

10:13 p.m.

Stan is sitting on my pillow like something out of a
fairy tale. I hope he's not thinking about turning into
a prince. I would not be okay with that.

SATURDAY OCTOBER 9

10:46 p.m. Home

Almost time to go to Nightshade Glade and I've got a bad case of THE DREADS.

Part of me is super up for some midnight-y, magic-y, moonlight-y mayhem, but a bigger part of me is super FREAKING OUT. What did Dad say last night? Write a list of the things that are worrying you and you'll see they're not so bad.... It's worth a try, I guess.

Things That Are ESPECIALLY Worrying Me RIGHT NOW

1. The risk of not getting off the ground. I ~~may~~ have messed up a bit on forward-planning

by bringing a frog home and not a broomstick because I can now confirm that ordinary kitchen brooms/brushes/ mops do not fly. Not even the vacuum. Nope. Zero enchantment + zero witch skills = zero levitation.*
I know this because I tried them all (which was embarrassing when Dad spotted me in the yard astride a mop, snorted, and asked if I was "still playing *pretend-horsey*" which was a) not funny and b) a bit much coming from the grown man who'd bought a spacehopper).

2. *If* I get off the ground, the risk that I'll get lost and/or stranded.

3. *If* lost and/or stranded in the forest, risk that I'll be eaten by a wolf. (Or other munchy creature hiding in the trees. A *werewolf*?? More interesting, but also probably more deadly.)

4. *If*, against the odds, I reach Nightshade Glade, the risk of messing up the spell/incantation/

*Practically math.

magic dance/digging part of the evening.

This risk is very high. Possibly also deadly.

Yep, still freaking out. *Anywhoo*, almost time to go.

10:55 p.m.

Have panic-eaten half a packet of sandwich cookies.
Feel a bit sick.

Okay, I don't have time to waste sitting around
eating. I don't even have time to sit around
panicking and I definitely don't have time to
be writing this diary.

10:59 p.m.

Finished the cookies. Must just triple-check my
checklist.

- ☑ 1 **flashlight**
- ☑ 1 **shovel**

☑ 1 bag for life (to put freshly dug-up skeledrake root in)
☑ ~~Many cookies~~ (eaten)
☑ 1 ~~creature strong in fang~~ frog
☐ 1 broomstick

All that's left is to stop at the school on my way and borrow a broomstick. Simple.

11:00 p.m.

Is it simple though?

I really need to get going!

SUNDAY OCTOBER 10

1:32 a.m. Home

On the upside, I'm back in my bedroom.

On the downside, I don't have any skeledrake root.

On the double-downside, I think that might be the least of my worries....

At first, everything seemed to be going according to plan. The school looked even more like a haunted castle than usual in the moonlight. I pushed the door open ... and almost fell over with shock. Staring back at me in the dark were rows of tiny, glittery eyes! **Croak, ribbit, croak.** Thankfully, it was only the left-behind class frogs watching me from their nighttime cubbyholes and hailing their adventurous fellow frog, Stan-the-Man. There was no sign of Mrs. Slater.

All good.

I slip-slid across the marble floor to the broom coat closet and two minutes later I was back outside, trying to find room on the broomstick for a shovel, a flashlight, a bag, a frog, and me.

"**Nightshade Glade**, please," I asked my broom as if it were a friendly bus conductor, and with a grumpy lurch it was off. Within seconds, I was over the twisty chimneys. *WHOOOOSH!* A sharp left and I was over the treetops.

TRAGICALLY, it turns out that flying over—and then, when the broom dropped down, *through*—a forest when you're not sure where you're going, the batteries in your flashlight have run out, and the moon keeps going behind clouds, is nothing like flying over the sports pitch. I had several nasty run-ins with branches that seemed to come out of nowhere, a trio of owls, and something unidentifiable but very spiky. *Anyway*, I'm not entirely sure how I got there, but I finally landed in the glade. The moon had come out again and I could see that someone—probably Miss

Lupo—had recently taped a big sign to the trunk of the twistiest elm:

Get Your Skeledrakes Here!

B-but ... where was everyone?

Where was *anyone?* I must have made up more time on the broom than I'd thought, but it was a little odd that I hadn't seen a single witch on the way here. Still, I wasn't going to hang aaround waiting for them. I was a relatively small and extremely USELESS witch person, and I seriously wanted to get out of this forest (*what even were those howling sounds?*), but more to the point, I'd have been crazy to wait for an audience for my original song-and-dance routine!

With a heartfelt apology to the Frost Moon, I filled my lungs and warbled:

"Oh, Frost Moon,
Oh, Moon of Frost,
You gleam so bright,
I cannot get lost."

I couldn't really blame it for going behind a cloud at that exact moment. Taking advantage of the darkness, I threw in some ~~classy~~ dance moves, twirling and bowing in the direction of the tangliest bushes to honor the forest spirits.

> "Oh, Frost Moon,
> You shine above,
> Tralalala,
> The Goddess of Love,"

I trilled mid-pirouette and Stan added a couple of **ribbits** to the mix.

> "Tralalalala....
> Lalala...."

I couldn't remember the next line (probably for the best) so I really went for it with some original shimmying—all those hours watching dance shows with Dad were really paying off! Stan was doing his very best to partner me, hopping around like his little froggy life depended on it. This was more fun than I thought it would be.

It was the noise that made me look up.

Ahhhhhhhhh! Stan leaped onto my shoulder and we both looked heavenwards and PANICKED. What was *that*?

Skimming over the treetops was not a grateful lunar spirit but a fizzing, spitting FIREBALL.

Wait ... TWO fireballs ... no ... one of them was a CAT and the other ... was my principal!

"*What. Do. You. Think. You. Are. Doing?*"

"Um—" There was a *looonnnng*, painful pause. "D-d-dancing?"

Ms. Sparks landed and said she could see that and for a second I thought she was going to laugh. But no. *Nooooo.* She was very, very upset. So upset that she wasn't just sparks by name: There was a halo of angry, fiery specks all around her head!

"WHAT. ARE. YOU. DOING. IN. THE. MIDDLE. OF. THE. NIGHT. IN. THE. FOREST?"

I tried to explain that I was digging up skeledrake roots, but she seemed to think this was a very poor explanation. "*WHAT ARE SKELEDRAKES?*" Why was she asking *me*? She was going to set fire to a tree if she didn't calm down. I tried to ignore the fact that a sheepish frog was now doing his  best to hide down the back of my shirt collar— *ughhhhhh*—and blurted out that I was just collecting ingredients for my potions homework. It might have been the truth, but it didn't impress her. It really was bad luck that she'd showed up *and* nobody else had.

"But how did you—" I began, but she didn't let me answer before she told me if I was going to the forest to BREAK SCHOOL RULES (*ooops*) it was a TERRIBLE idea to stop off at school on the way.

"But it was in her notes—" I began, and Ms. Sparks stopped asking WHY and started asking WHAT NOTES? And WHOSE NOTES? *Tricky.*

"Hand them over," she demanded, fixing me with such a Steely Glare I looked away and caught Zephyr's eye instead (big mistake: that cat was terrifying). I stood there, my mouth opening and closing like a goldfish. I might be in DEEP trouble, but something told me that handing over these notes wasn't going to make anything any easier.

"Great giggling GOATS," began Ms. Sparks.

What now? My pocket was twitching like it was home to a ferret....

"Give me those NOTES!"

Out flew the notes and I watched, cringing, as they turned a show-offy somersault in the air and landed neatly in the open mouth of the little gold handbag propped on the end of the principal's broom. "Okay," she said as the handbag snapped itself shut with a superior *tut*, "I'll see you in my office Monday morning at nine o'clock. Sharp."

And that was that. With a single wave of her wand, I was back on my borrowed broom, and in what felt like an instant, back here in my bedroom, writing this down because there is no way I'm getting to sleep. Too much to worry about.

Will I get a detention?

Will I get suspended?

Will I get expelled? Ex*SPELLED*?

Not sure how I feel about that.

1:52 a.m.

I keep thinking about Blair's notes. Did she make a mistake? There must be an explanation.

2:33 a.m.

There IS a possible explanation, but it's not very nice....

2:55 a.m.

Could it really have been a joke??? Right now, it doesn't feel very funny.

8:59 p.m.

Today has been a very BAD day.

And *no*, Dad's persistent attempts to find out what was wrong with me and then cheer me up by a) saying every five minutes, "Whatever it is, it can't be *that* bad!" (wrong) and b) feeding me a burned grilled cheese sandwich didn't help.

Not even FLUFFMALLOWS helped.

MONDAY OCTOBER 11

8:58 a.m. School

So here I am, back outside the principal's office ... *in for it*. Again.

Blair's inside right now, and even though I can't hear exactly what Ms. Sparks is saying, I can tell she's NOT happy. I don't think Blair's very happy, either, but she doesn't seem to be getting a word in.

She was already waiting when I arrived and I was just winding myself up to ask her WHY she'd sent me off into the deep, dark forest in the middle of the night on my own* to dig up skeledrakes (what even *were* they?) when she greeted me with, "Witches that snitches end up in ditches," and catapulted a **GO** ball straight over my head and into a large nearby urn

*Except for a frog.

full of daisies and a family of visiting toads.

The good news was that none of the toads
(which are still hopping angrily around my ankles)
was harmed, but the bad news was that now I felt
a) guilty and b) a little worried that that was an
actual SPELL. So I told her that I hadn't snitched to
Ms. Sparks and I hadn't *meant* to hand over the notes.
It had just *happened*.

I don't know if she believed me because all she
said was, "I wish I'd seen your original dance."

Um ... *was she trying not to laugh*?

"Did the Frost Moon LOVE it?" She was definitely
laughing! And then Stan (who was meant to be here
for moral support) started shaking in exactly the way
I'd expect a frog to shake if a frog could get a fit of the
giggles. Traitor!

"What about the song?" Blair snorted. "Did the tree
spirits join in?"

Were the TOADS laughing at me now, too? This
was the opposite of funny *except* ... there's something
very catching about giggles when you're in trouble.

"You could have just gotten me back," she said, but before I could stop snickering and ask her for any helpful tips on revenge, Zephyr put her head around the door, followed a second later by Ms. Sparks, and no one was laughing anymore.

9:11 a.m.

Blair just came out—nope, definitely not laughing now.

"Your turn," she says, glaring at me. "Have fun."

GULP.

9:31 a.m.

Well, that was odd.

Ms. Sparks didn't give me cookies this time. Instead, she gave me a very long and painful LECTURE. So now I know:

1. Skeledrake root is not a thing. Apparently, even a **toadbrain** would know that (she didn't put it quite like that).

2. It would be most unusual for a sixth grade potion to need ingredients that could not be found a) in the school yards, b) on the shelves of the lab or c) in Mr. Riggle's Emporium on Main Street.

3. The forest was very dangerous at night and not a place to be "prancing around" on my own. I asked her what the howling noises were and she said that it wasn't a good time to "PANIC me any further."

4. For future reference, frogs are NOT creatures strong in fang.* Zephyr seemed to find that particular misunderstanding very funny.

5. Ms. Sparks didn't say anything about Blair's notes, but she did suggest that it was good to keep an open mind, but not so open that my brain fell out.

Then she asked me, in a much kinder voice, whether I was finally getting the hang of levitation. I said "sort of," which was a lie. She seemed happy

*It didn't seem like the right moment to ask her about puppies.

because apparently levitation was an early witch skill to "come in," and once I had that under my belt, the sky was the limit. Haha.

It was my punishment that was the really ODD part. I haven't been expelled or suspended or even got a detention. Instead, I've been ordered to join the *Junior Halloween Ball Committee*. This makes NO sense. PARTY PLANNING? I mean, I like parties (or at least I used to before I became someone whose favorite place to hang out was a broom closet and whose best friend was a frog). It doesn't sound *that* bad ... but then nothing at this school ever turns out to be the way it sounds.

9:45 a.m.

Apparently, Blair's punishment is to clean out all the frog cubicles without using magic for the rest of the year. She's still not laughing. I don't think she's talking to me anymore, either. Amara says she's really lucky to still be **Queen of Mischief** and that Ms. Sparks must have forgotten about it. I don't think Blair is feeling "really lucky"—she doesn't seem to be a big frog fan. I don't think she'll ever show me how to do loop-the-loops now.

1:11 p.m.

A very neat and detailed, color-coded, and highlighted schedule was sitting on my desk after lunch. The Post-it note stuck to the front read:

I was already panicking when Hunter walked past, looked over my shoulder and drawled, "I wouldn't go on THAT committee if you paid me— not with *her* in charge. She's a tyrant, like literally the bossiest witch in the school." He shuddered theatrically. "Good luck."

On second thought, I wouldn't mind cleaning out the frog cubbyholes with Blair.

7:02 p.m. Home

I accidentally told Dad I'd joined the Halloween Ball planning committee and now he thinks I'm super EXCITED and *finally* making an effort to try to settle into my new school. He looks so happy and relieved I don't have the heart to tell him it's *not quite like that.*

He's now halfway through a very embarrassing story about him falling into a cake at a party when he was my age. Sometimes I worry.

"The costume I'm making for you is going to be AMAZING by the way," he says.

Changing schools, preferably before HALLOWEEN, is now CRITICAL.

8:45 p.m.

I'm sitting in bed, having a practice, one-person brainstorming session. I want to make the right impression at tomorrow's committee meeting so they don't think I'm the most useless **toadbrain** of all useless **toadbrains**. Also, I'm frightened of the TYRANT-IN-CHARGE.

Okay. I need a proper list like a proper, organized, brain-stormy kind of ~~witch~~ person.

<u>FOOD</u>

(NOT made by Mr. Scary Cook and as non-witchy as possible)

- Tons of crispy things (like chips)
- Cookies (must inc. Oreos)
- Cupcakes (do I have time to learn to BAKE????)
- Something special for the frogs to eat??? (NOT fish sticks)

<u>PARTY MUST-HAVES</u>

- Playlist
- Disco ball????

HALLOWEEN VIBES

- Fake candles
- Pumpkin-carving station?
- Apple bobbing
- Station for fake, Halloweeny makeup!
- Fake bats/bat decorations??
- Fake skeletons
- Fake spiders' webs

It is an EPIC list, so fingers crossed the committee president doesn't eat me alive (although that would be very Halloweeny).

Zoology homework:
Read Chapter 4 of Ambius Ambrose's Animalium Magicum.

TUESDAY OCTOBER 12

1:55 p.m. School

Okay, so I've just come out of the meeting and it was
NOT what I was expecting.

The scary-TYRANT-committee-
chair was only Winnie ~~Boss~~
Ross! It's true that she had
three clipboards, one of those
little hammer things judges
have, and a MEGAPHONE
(which she was not afraid to use), but
she's always been nice to me. Puck and Amara and
Fabi are all on the committee—I didn't ask if they'd
been forced to sign up, too.

Winnie was happy I'd made a list (she *really*

likes lists), and she lent me a clipboard *and the megaphone* so I could read it to the whole committee. But ... it turns out witches do Halloween and parties *slighhhhtllyyyyy* differently. First of all, I offended everyone with my list of shop-bought food.

"Why would we eat that?" Amara seemed genuinely confused. "Mr. Cook makes the best party cakes in the world."

I remembered the sausages and shuddered.

Puck lobbed a mini cupcake at me.

Okay, it looked delicious, it even smelled good, but I wasn't going to make the same mistake twice. No witch food was ever going to cross my lips again. I palmed it off on Stan as discreetly as I could and moved on.

By the time I got to the end of my list, everyone was laughing, literally rolling around on the floor, snorting and snickering.

"First off," Winnie said after she'd finally stopped laughing and taken back her megaphone, "you can cross out all the *fakes*."

I was confused and said that obviously we couldn't have *real* skeletons?!

That went down very badly. Apparently, it's Indiana's favorite night of the whole year. Who is Indiana, you might ask? I certainly did. Well, it's INDIANA BONES—the live skeleton (well, *probably* not actually *live*, but you know what I mean) who lives in the senior science lab.

"And why would we need FAKE Halloween makeup?" asked Amara, rolling her eyes. "Demo time." She wiggled her wand, said a little chant, and just like that, her skin turned bright orange.

Apple bobbing was another no-no—teen witches in costume, explained Puck, shaking his long hair like a wet dog, were not overly thrilled with sticking their heads in buckets.

"*Wait....*" Winnie, who'd grabbed my list and was crossing things out furiously, paused, pen in hand, "the bat decorations are not a TERRIBLE idea."

I started to feel smug, but then a witch from seventh

grade named Fred said it was a BASIC and ORDINARY idea and everyone except me nodded.

"True," said Winnie, "but real bats are a NIGHTMARE at parties."

More enthusiastic nodding and I joined in this time, because even though I'd never met a real bat at a party, I couldn't *imagine* they were great guests.

"They can get a little *hyper*," admitted Puck, who was hanging upside down from the curtain pole at the time.

"Yeah, they always drink too much punch and get hysterical," added Fabi.

"So? How does it work?" Amara (who was now only thirty percent tangerine) asked me. "We spell some decorations?"

"Noooooo!" I said. "We MAKE it. It's not hard." I crossed my fingers. I might not know *exactly* how to make bat decorations, but I had no idea how to SPELL it.* "It'll be fun."

They all looked at me like I'd suggested cleaning

*Or anything else.

out the frogs, but then Winnie said that it was important to be open to new ways of doing things, however *backward*, and that anyway I needed something to be busy with that wasn't too *demanding*. I would have been offended except that a) she was totally right and b) she high-fived me when she said it.

So my official job—announced by megaphone and recorded in the meeting minutes—is now **Witch In Charge Of Bat Decorations.**

7:01 p.m. Home

Dad's been home for a while, but it looks like I'm making dinner. He has locked himself in the yard shed and won't let me in. "It will spoil the surprise!" he shouted through the door.

I've had too many surprises in the last few weeks. I HATE surprises now.

7:33 p.m.

Toast for dinner it is. I have a lot to do.

HOW TO MAKE BAT DECORATIONS

- Find a picture of a bat and then copy its shape on to a piece of card or paper. This might take a few tries (don't give up if early attempts look like pigeons or manta rays or tents).

- OR ... you could trace over this helpful bat template right here....

- Halloween bats are traditionally black, but if orange or purple bats are your thing, go for it. Feel free to stick big, googly eyes on your bats, too. Glitter or neon stripes can also add to the Halloween vibe.

- Make TONS of bats and then carefully hole-punch the edges of each bat's wings and string them all together with thick black thread or cord.

8:45 p.m.

Operation Bat Decorations is underway!

FRIDAY OCTOBER 15

8:33 p.m. Home

Sixteen days to Halloween. Very busy.

The good news is I got nine out of twenty on my potions test. Okay, not *that* good, but it could have been much worse. Puck got three out of twenty. It's true that my very smelly potion did not work AT ALL, but Miss Lupo said my crushing and mixing were satisfactory *and* that it was surprisingly TASTY. At least it wasn't a spot-*making* potion like Puck's.

The bad news is so BAD it hurts to write it down. Today's GO score....

DODOS: 0

DRAGONS: 141

I don't know if it makes it better or worse, but what I *and everyone else wearing a yellow Dodo bib* say is that balls don't just "jump back out" of the chimney EVERY SINGLE TIME without FOUL PLAY. Ms. Celery says she didn't see anything (????) and if we suspected cheating then we should "get off our butts and use our wands." I'm not sure what she meant by that, but I'm beginning to think that what gets you into trouble at witch school is not always the same as at ordinary school.

The Dragons were VERY SMUG. Blair did an entire circuit of loop-the-loops to celebrate. She really is annoyingly good on a broomstick.

Bat Decoration Tally: 37 (would have been more but it's hard to concentrate on cutting out bats after your team's been DESTROYED).

SATURDAY OCTOBER 16

4:43 p.m. Taffy Tallywick's Teashop
Fifteen days 'til **Halloween.**

Winnie called an Emergency Saturday Committee Meeting, which is why I'm sitting in the teashop, with the kitten on my feet, taking the minutes.

1. Clean the **Great Hall**.
2. Clean and polish all 107 of the special silver **Halloween** cake stands and all 33 of the special golden punchbowls.

I just saw Ash and some of his friends walking past the window! I gave him a little awkward wave and

he gave a little awkward wave back and then one of the boys he was with said something to him and he turned red. Amara asked me if he was the boy I'd tried to introduce her to in Rhubarb & Custard, and when I said he was, she gave a little awkward wave, too, but Ash pretended he didn't see her and started walking faster.

"Does your friend go to the **Academy**?" asked Winnie.

"Yes, and he's really nice," I said firmly.

They all looked at each other until Winnie declared it was time to get back to business.

People in this town need to get a grip.

Anyway, where was I?

3. Ask Mr. Zicasso for more black cardstock and glue from the art-room supplies.
4. Arrange a small gold throne for Zephyr. *Seriously?*
5. Clean the Great Chandelier.

It's beginning to dawn on me that the Junior Committee's responsibilities involve A LOT of cleaning.

Bat Decoration Tally: 59 (would have been sixty but Puck spilled hot chocolate on one).

SUNDAY OCTOBER 17

7:13 p.m. Home

Went over to Ash's house to see if I could borrow some glue. Neither of us mentioned Taffy Tallywick's, but when I asked if we could hang out during the holiday break he said, "Definitely!" His mom had just finished cutting his hair, and his bangs are now so terrifyingly straight that he looks like a Lego figure. Anyway, I was glad I managed not to laugh because Mrs. Namdar asked me to stay for dinner and it was meatballs. Yum!

8:55 p.m.

Have stuck seventy-nine googly eyes on forty bats and I'm calling it a day.

Trying not to think about school tomorrow. *Obviously*, I'm dreading another day of failing TRAGICALLY at all things witchy, *but* there are only fourteen days 'til Halloween. So much to do! Must remember to get more GOOGLY EYES.

9:09 p.m.

Thinking about school tomorrow. ~~Slightly~~ Regretting not ~~finishing~~ starting my history homework.

Make a model of a medieval witch castle including potion laboratory, high walls for protection from Ordinaries, magical moat, Great Banqueting Hall, and broomstick landing pad.

MONDAY OCTOBER 18

9:01 a.m. School

Thirteen days 'til Halloween.

I asked Winnie how many decorations we'd need and she said at least twelve strings. I didn't think that sounded too bad until she added that each string should have at least A HUNDRED bats strung on it. I asked her if she was joking, but she asked me if I'd seen the size of the **Great Hall**.

1:55 p.m.

The **Great Hall** looks even GREATER with all the chairs packed away. Winnie's right: We're going to need *a lot of decorations*. Also, dusting this place is going to take us until *next* Halloween. I thought Winnie would just wave her wand, but apparently we're only allowed to do cleaning-up spells in class because Ms. Sparks says, "All Extraordinary witches must also learn to be competent at ordinary life skills," and that, "Broom skills don't start and stop with flying." Disappointing!

I pointed out all the cobwebs we'd have to clear to Winnie, but she just looked at me like I was a terrible person. She said that we had to ask their owners nicely and then clean *under* the webs—SPIDERS deserved to live here as much as the rest of us.

I suppose it kind of makes sense???

According to Winnie's clipboard, one of the teachers is going to take down the Great Chandelier for us this week so we can polish it.

I'd forgotten just how BIG that chandelier was.

7:32 p.m. Home

Bat Decoration Tally: 185. I've stepped up production. (I was hoping Dad would help, but he's locked himself in the shed again.)

THURSDAY OCTOBER 21

6:49 p.m. Home

A LOT happened on Tuesday, which meant that this diary needed a couple of days off to lie quietly in my sock drawer and recover.

I'd had a feeling things were going too smoothly. I should have known when I passed my fractions test (fourteen out of twenty, *woo-hoo*!) that my day had peaked. But in English, Madam Binx lulled me into a false sense of security. Literally.

"This spell will help you be at one with your inner-calm-witch," she announced in her singsong voice while watering her Venus flytrap. "It's one of my favorites."

I sighed so loudly everyone turned to look at me.

My inner-*anything*-witch had yet to show up.

"Mallowmoons," she murmured.
"Bibbblyblossommms. *Cllllllooooouddsss*."

My eyes were drooping (although that could have been because I'd stayed up all night punching holes in cardboard bat wings).

"A serene witch is a powerful witch because they are not wasting their energy on frenetic nonsense—IS THERE ANY REASON, PUCK BERRY," she yelled, "FOR YOU TO BE PUTTING THAT BAT DOWN FABI'S CLOAK?"

"It's not a real bat!" Puck said (it was one of my cut-out bats). "Even I wouldn't be stupid enough to bring a REAL bat into class."

Madam Binx tried to look upset, but she had a soft spot for Puck. "You all have a lot of work to do on your inner calm," she said, rolling her eyes. "Okay, sit quietly for two minutes and think soothing thoughts while I duck to Miss Lupo's room and borrow some lavender. That might help. I'm trusting you," she said and closed the door.

One minute Blair was sitting at her desk looking serene and the next minute, with a **WHOOSH**, she was standing beside me.

"Well, what do we have here? Bea's *diary*." And before I even knew what was happening, she was waving my diary—THIS DIARY—in the air. "*Ooooooh! Top secret.*" She snickered. "*Tuesday the twenty-first of September, one forty five. Woke up sweating. I'd had this* terrifying *nightmare that I'd gone to a school full of WITCHES and FROGS*," she read in a silly voice that I think was meant to sound like me.

I LAUNCHED myself at her and made a GRAB. Too late! She'd tossed my diary high in the air— up, up, up and *nooooooooo!* down, down ... *into the open jaws of Madam Binx's Venus flytrap....*

SNAP!

Some witches were laughing, but not all of them.
I didn't even care—I was too busy gulping back tears
and trying to persuade a POT PLANT to give me back
my diary.

It was Winnie who came to my rescue. "Spit it out!"
she said very firmly to the flytrap. The big plant shook
its spiky trap. "SPIT IT OUT AT ONCE! It's forgotten it's
carnivorous. AT ONCE!"

And finally, because it was hard to say no to
Winnie, with a huge BELCH, the flytrap burped back
out my diary and I scrambled to pick it up. The relief!

Winnie turned her fierce attention to Blair. "Too
far!" she said. "That was MEAN." Then she whipped
out her wand, waved it, whispered something ...
and absolutely nothing happened. Blair grinned
triumphantly—she'd gotten away with it.

Or had she?

"What's going on NOW!" Madam Binx had come
back into the room. "Honestly, you're the worst sixth-
grade group I've had in years." I had a bad feeling
that might be my fault. "Somebody fill me in please...."

Amara?" Miss Binx picked on the nearest witch and waggled her wand warningly. "Spill."

Amara shrugged and snitched.

"Explain yourself, Miss Smith-Smythe," said Madam Binx, and Blair tried. She really tried.

"It wa—" Blair burped. "B— *Burrp!* B-Bea's fa—" The lie got lost in another loud belch.

"Stop making those disgusting noises and tell me why you took another witch's private journal AND FED IT TO MY PET." Madam Binx was angry.

"*BURRRRP*," protested Blair. "I mean— *BELCH!*"

"You will write a four-hundred-word essay for me comparing the natural and magical diets of giant Venus flytraps and you will have it on my desk by first thing tomorrow morning." Wow, *really* angry.

"B-but, Mad— *Burp!* I—" Blair broke off and stared at Winnie, a look of complete outrage on her face. "Did you SP— *Buuuurrrrrrpppp!*"

Winnie Ross is a GENIUS! It's still making me snicker two days later, possibly because a) Blair was still burping today and b) my diary has finally dried out and (except for the flytrap toothmarks) is as good as new.

Only **ten days** 'til **Halloween** and I've still got 976 cardboard bats to cut out (would have been 971 except I accidentally set fire to some of them in physics).

11:10 a.m. School

GO is a crazy game. I was scoring a goal and fell down the chimney. When I rolled out, miraculously in one piece but covered in soot, all Winnie said was that I'd better get back out there because it was a tight match.

Final score:

DODOS: 99	DRAGONS: 98

Blair is still popping out mini-burps when she least expects it, which is the only possible excuse for the SHOCKING FOUL she did on Fabi.

He's covered in cat-shaped bandages but I don't think he minds too much because WE WON!!

2:55 p.m.

It was Madam Binx's turn to give the Friday lecture, and because of what she referred to as "recent events," her chosen subject was WITCH JOURNALING. It was, she said with a stern look in the direction of where sixth grade was sitting, an important witch skill that should be treated with *respect*.

"A journal can be not only a written record of your path as a witch, however *bumpy* that path might be –" this time she smiled straight at me—"but a place you can record your thoughts and feelings, especially after rituals or any other special happenings in your magical life. Every witch should have one."

Blair, who was sitting right behind me (which was a shame because I'd been trying very hard to keep out of her way), leaned forward and whispered in my ear, "Witch journal? Ha! (*tiny burp*) You won't need one of those ... just an ORDINARY (*hiccup*) journal for you, Bea Black."

Hunter, who was sitting next to her, laughed.

And after that, even though Madam Binx was saying a lot of really interesting things about mind maps and daily motivations and sticking in cake recipes and autumn leaves, etc. etc., I couldn't concentrate. For someone who never asked to be a witch, I feel surprisingly BAD to be told I'm not one.

The Extraordinary: Halloween Issue 2

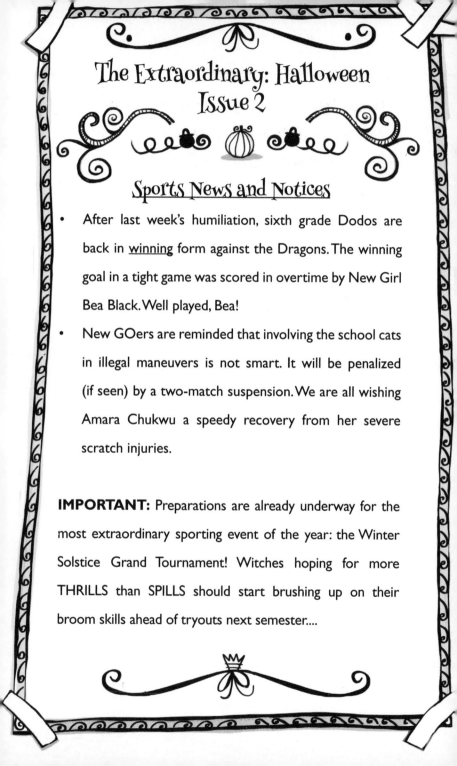

Sports News and Notices

- After last week's humiliation, sixth grade Dodos are back in <u>winning</u> form against the Dragons. The winning goal in a tight game was scored in overtime by New Girl Bea Black. Well played, Bea!

- New GOers are reminded that involving the school cats in illegal maneuvers is not smart. It will be penalized (if seen) by a two-match suspension. We are all wishing Amara Chukwu a speedy recovery from her severe scratch injuries.

IMPORTANT: Preparations are already underway for the most extraordinary sporting event of the year: the Winter Solstice Grand Tournament! Witches hoping for more THRILLS than SPILLS should start brushing up on their broom skills ahead of tryouts next semester....

Other Notices

Mrs. Slater would like to remind all students that the Halloween Ball will end promptly at <u>10 p.m.</u> There is to be no repeat of last year's post-ball shenanigans.

Quick-fire Q & A with Mr. Muddy!

Q: Favorite meal?

A: Sausages.

Q: Favorite teacher?

A: *Long pause while Mr. Muddy blushes and refuses to answer so we're going to say Miss Lupo*

Q: Favorite joke?

A: What's it like to be kissed by a vampire? It's a pain in the neck!

Thank you, Mr. Muddy! That joke was TERRIBLE.

Dear Agony Witch

Dear Agony Witch,

I'm a new girl and I can't do any magic. I am useless at everything, and although everyone in my class is very kind, I'm sure nobody likes me.

Yours,

A Worried New Girl

I DID NOT WRITE THIS!!!!

THURSDAY OCTOBER 28

8:32 p.m. Home
Three days 'til Halloween!!!

Very busy day. Had my lunch in the lunchroom
with the rest of the Committee. Obviously, I took in
my own food because of my no-witch-
food-ever-again rule, and even
though they all thought my
jam sandwiches were some
kind of bloody **Halloween** prop,
they didn't FORCE me to share their
sausages.

Jam, not blood.

Spent PD cleaning the Great Chandelier,
again. It is getting very sparkly, and although the
spiders are a little annoyed about having to move out

of our way while we polish, and some of them are very large, I think it's going very well.

Bat Decoration Tally: 921!!! Mr. Zicasso let the whole class help in art on Tuesday. Blair might not be my Favorite person, but I have to admit she's very quick at cutting out bats. (Hunter said it was a complete accident that he spilled glue on my seat. Sure.)

FRIDAY OCTOBER 29

11:03 a.m. School
Two days 'til Halloween!!!!

WILD morning.

Puck said he'd teach me the hair-color-changing ~~trick~~ spell. I wanted to go temporarily yellow for PE because I'm very committed to being a Dodo, but his demo went wrong. I didn't even have a chance to get my wand out before he'd given me one cat-shaped patch of neon GREEN on my head. He offered to fix it but a) I thought I might end up with no head at all and b) Ms. Celery was calling us onto the pitch.

Also ... I don't exactly *hate* it.

Final score:

DODOS: 190   DRAGONS: 100

Best game ever. I scored SEVEN goals! Puck chalked it up to the "lucky cat" on my head. *Obviously*, that had nothing to do with it (but just in case, I'm keeping it).

5:35 p.m. Home

Dad is freaking out about my hair. He's mostly annoyed that I denied dyeing it, which was not fair because I was actually telling the truth!

"Well, how else did it turn that *interesting* shade?" he asked. I couldn't come up with a fib on the spot, so instead I reminded him he'd said it was good to stand out. That went down as well as could be expected.

5:55 p.m.

Ash came over with some cookies his mom had baked. I think she worries about us.

I wonder if she'd teach me how to make these

cookies. They're named koloocheh and they're very pretty but more importantly, VERY delicious.

Ash couldn't stop snorting every time he noticed my hair (it's hard to miss).

 ### 6:12 p.m.

Koloocheh for dinner. Fabulous.

9:33 p.m.

Bat Decoration Tally: *still* 921. Never ever want to see another bat in my life, and I have 279 more to make before lunchtime tomorrow!!

SATURDAY OCTOBER 30 (HALLOWEEN EVE!!!!!)

3:21 p.m. School

School feels so odd on the weekend! Fewer witches but more cats.

Today's the last day the Junior Committee is allowed into the **Great Hall**. At midnight, the students and teachers on the Senior Ball Committee take over and add what Winnie calls a "few surprises." So we've all been polishing and sweeping and stringing decorations* since DAWN, and not gonna lie, I think we've done an AMAZING job. The hall is SPARKLING, with every single cobweb intact. All the polished cake stands and shiny punchbowls have been returned to Mr. Scary Cook, Zephyr's gold

*1,188 bats, which is close enough for even Winnie to be happy.

throne is by the fireplace, and the Great Chandelier is blinding! But we're all FILTHY and STARVING so we're off to Taffy Tallywick's to recover.

8:50 p.m. Home

Nervous but also more excited about the party tomorrow than I thought I would be. I hope everyone likes the decorations. As long as nobody forces me to dance, it should be fine.

I have the weirdest feeling I'm forgetting something I should be worrying about....

SUNDAY OCTOBER 31 (HALLOWEEEEENNNN!!!!!)

5:01 p.m. Home

"Ta-da!" says Dad. "Look what I made!"

I don't say anything, mostly because my jaw is on the floor.

"It's for YOU!"

NOOOOOOOO! I've remembered what I should have been worrying about. My costume.

"Stop scribbling in that diary for once and say something!"

Um....

5:15 p.m.

"It's ... WOW!" I managed at last. "It's so GREEN!"

Dad nodded happily. It was VERY green.

"It's a FROG!" He was so proud. "I know you didn't want to dress up as a WITCH and you love frogs."

I gulped—"it" was a very BIG, *suspiciously spacehopper-sized* FROG costume. Dad set it down on the floor, and with a flourish, produced a bright green T-shirt and a pair of tights, neon-green face paint, and some googly, froggy eyes *boinging* around on a headband. "The finishing touches!"

He was not wrong. I was FINISHED.

"And I know it's not *anatomically correct*," he said, as if the rest was, "but I added a handy pouch to the front for snacks or whatever you carry around with you ... a hairbrush? Lip gloss?"

A hairbrush wasn't going to help. *Lip gloss* wasn't going to help! To be fair, snacks might. Where were the emergency cookies?

6:21 p.m.

I am standing by my bed, DESPAIRING. I would be lying face down on my bed, DESPAIRING, if it wasn't for the sad fact that I *can't* lie down.

I am IN the frog costume. I am *Bea-frogged.*

What. Am. I. Going. To. Do? This is one of the most serious and terrible crises of my entire life (which is why, even in the DEPTHS of my despair, I am writing it all down).

If I wear this costume, it will mean social death.

But if I don't wear it, I might make Dad CRY.

6:25 p.m.

Through my sweaty panic, I could vaguely hear someone calling my name, and a second later a soccer ball **WHOOSHED** through my open window. Ash was trying to get my attention. I'd definitely gotten *his* attention—he had tears running down his face.

"It is NOT FUNNY!" I yelled, lobbing the ball back and narrowly missing him. Shame.

"It kind of *is*," he snorted. He laughed so much he almost fell out of the window (which would have served him right). "Have fun, though!" he shouted and grinned, and I couldn't help but grin back even though IT IS NOT FUNNY.

6:32 p.m.

Okay. I have a solution.

I will leave the house in Full Frog and get changed in the forest. I can hide some leggings in the pouch, *and diary, too!* although even if I had to go to the ball in my underwear, that would be an improvement.

6:38 p.m.

Dad is driving me to school! He is being completely UNREASONABLE—no matter what I say I can't persuade him to let me walk through the forest in the dark dressed as a frog.

My life is over.

7:13 p.m. School

I'm having a little moment in a coat closet while I calm down. The last five minutes have been TRAUMATIC.

We pulled up in front of the school and Dad (who was overexcited because there was a minor meteor shower over the chimneys) *rolled me* off the back seat like a ... well, spacehopper. Sadly, we were not alone. There were orange bubble cars everywhere dropping off witches. Witches ready to party, witches in perfect costumes that can only be achieved with some serious wand-work ... witches in perfect *witch costumes....*

Nooooooo.

Slinky witches and fluorescent witches and witches in saris, crinoline-wearing witches with pointy hats and witches in velvet flares and witches in head-to-toe black Lycra with stripes on their capes. Everyone was wearing black—shiny black or glittery black or black with feathers, but only black. Even all the cats were black. There were witches on roller skates and witches on stilts. *There was even a small witch in a ragged cloak with very realistic warts.*

What there wasn't was a single witch-as-a-FROG—or witch-as-anything-but-witch. And nobody was green.

Dad and I looked at each other. "Oh, well," he said with a guilty shrug, turning the key in the ignition. "It's good to stand out." And then he was off!

He wasn't the only one who made a speedy getaway. I took one look at the growing crowd of witches-as-witches, pointing and *oohing* at me, and ran as fast as I could—not that fast in this costume—to the nearest available broom closet.

7:17 p.m.

Wait, I have my wand in my pouch! This would be a really good time to discover if I can finally do magic....

7:21 p.m.

Okay, I still can't do magic, but I now have a small singed hole in the middle of my huge frog bum and I've eaten all my snacks.

I'm not having a good time.

7:23 p.m.

Maybe I could steal one of these broomsticks and fly away to somewhere like the Galapagos Islands (??) where they might appreciate human-sized frogs?

No one will miss m⸺

11:29 p.m. Home

SPOILER! The Halloween Ball is over and I'm still alive.

It was Winnie and Puck who came to get me. They almost fell over at the FROGGINESS of me, but they recovered quickly and then literally took the pen out of my hand and *dragged* me out of the broom closet.

"You're not missing tonight, Bea," said Winnie so fiercely that several of the floofy things decorating her witch's hat fell off.

"Wouldn't be the same without you, Hoppy!" shouted Puck, tugging me in the direction of the party, the music getting louder as we approached.

Oh, my broomstick! Being on the Junior Ball Committee had not prepared me for THIS!

"Apple and toffee?" Unless I was going crazy,* two of the silvery birch trees that usually stood at the entrance to the school had ... somehow ... *relocated* to stand at the entrance to the **Great Hall** and were ... *serving drinks.* *"Or strudel and coffee?"* The nearest tree adjusted one of the bow ties attached to his lower branches. "U-u-mm, apple and t-toffee?" I stammered and he ladled punch from a bowl hanging off another of his branches into a small red crystal glass.

"Happy Halloween!" He presented the cup to me with a flourish and ushered me into the hall. *"I'm sure it will be a night to remember."* He was not wrong.

It was like walking into a CAULDRON!**

The Great Chandelier was gleaming and glimmering with zillions of tiny red candles, and the

*Not impossible.
**IN A GOOD WAY!!

spiders we'd very carefully not dusted away were busy weaving and re-weaving their silk threads in intricate patterns between the layers of lights so that new pictures constantly appeared and disappeared in shadows on the walls—leaping cats and dueling vampires and prancing unicorns and more!

A DJ booth was floating on a magic carpet above the dance floor, surarounded by glittering disco balls twirling in mid-air. Behind the decks, Mr. Muddy in a scary-scientist-witch costume, assisted by Indiana Bones, was busting out "Thriller."

In one corner of the hall, some crab apples were fluttering around on tiny leaf wings ("the witch version of apple bobbing," explained Puck) and on the other side of the room a small gaggle of witches and their cats were toasting marshmallows over one of the flaming torches attached to the wall.

Up above, the bat decorations, *my bat decorations*, were hanging in loops crisscrossing the ceiling, swaying gently in a breeze no one could feel, so that it really did look like they were flying! Not gonna lie: I felt PROUD, but ... while *I* might be looking at strings of paper bats, I was suddenly *very* aware that everyone else was looking at *me*.

There were at least a hundred costumed witches in here and I was *still* the only FROG. There were *actual* frogs, of course—the class frogs were doing an acrobatics display on a golden table under the chandelier, and Stan, hiding at the back, was looking from the costume to me, and back again, with a look of HORROR on his little froggy face.

"I'm sorry," I mouthed at him, trying to ignore the fact I was now surarounded by a small crowd of pointing witches.

"Wow!" It was Hunter's voice. I had literally stopped a conga in its tracks. "That is *some* costume." I had a feeling that was not a compliment. Hunter poked me in my papier-mâché stomach. "WOW!" he said again. "I don't know how you did it, but ... *cool.*"

Then someone started to clap. And, one by one, all the other witches—in their annoyingly perfect WITCH costumes—joined in.

I was DEAD.

"That. Is. Amazing." Fabi broke out of the conga line and loped over. "And it matches your hair! What spell did you use?"

I mumbled that I hadn't spelled it, that my dad had made it.

There was a collective *gasp.*

"He MADE it?!" Fabi's eyes widened. "Like, with his *hands*? And, like, not a *wand*?"

I turned red under the green face paint and shook my head.

"No magic at all?" Hunter raised one eyebrow. "I don't believe you."

"Is he an artist?" whispered a small witch in a

black lace cape, with a glittery witch's hat over her headscarf.

"So cool, so *avant-garde*." Mr. Zicasso (in black sequins) had zoomed over now and was considering me from every angle like I was an original work by Da Vinciwick.

"And there's a pouch!" squealed Madam Binx, floating over to have a closer look. "I do love a costume with pockets."

"You're the first witch who's come as something other than A WITCH for a hundred and thirty-three years." Gilbert Swizz, *a senior*, sauntered over and nodded approvingly, sending a ripple of impressed whispers around the crowd. *Approvingly?*

Wait ... it was dawning on me ... my costume was a HIT!

"Would your dad make one for me next year?" asked a random ninth grader.

"Can he do any other animals?" asked another. "Like an elephant?"

"A duck-billed platypus?" Suggestions were

coming fast and furious.

"An axolotl?" That was Puck.

I nodded manically, googly eyes boinging around on my head.

"Okay, witches!" Mr. Muddy came out from behind the decks. "Let Bea sample the delights of her first **Halloween Ball!**"

"Dance with us, Bea!" Amara (who had gone full witchy witch with long golden chin hairs and *striped socks*) was already pulling me toward the throng of witches in the middle of the room.

"Maybe later." I hung back. Unless I was alone in the forest in the dark, I found dancing *challenging,* and they all seemed to know the complicated steps to a song I'd never heard before.

"Cupakes, then," Amara said happily, and before I knew what I was doing, we were heading at full speed—Puck and Winnie and Fabi, too—toward a long table at the side of the hall set with our 107 gleaming, towering cake stands, the 33 punchbowls, candelabras, flowers, and glimmering crystals and surrounded by a little crowd already munching away. Everyone looked happy enough, but what I wanted to know was *why was there smoke coming out of their noses and ears??*

Puck grabbed what looked like a red velvet cupcake and took a huge bite. POOOOFFFFF! Little puffs of sparkly blue steam shot out of his ears. Winnie took a big bite out of what might have been a brownie. WHOOSH! Red steam puffed out of her nostrils. She giggled.

"Try one, Bea!"

Nooooooo, not witch food!

But Puck was already advancing with a cupcake, and before I could duck my mouth was full of— OH! The first bite tasted like the crispiest apple, but as soon as I swallowed there was a loud PUFF, my ears were streaming green smoke, and the bite of cupcake burst into the most delicious warm liquid toffee I'd ever tasted in my life!

But at the exact moment I was falling in love with **Witch Halloween**, the doors to the hall burst open and Izzi appeared, walking backward. "BEHOLD, the QUEEEN of MISCHIEFFFFF is in the house!" she announced.

Blair Smith-Smythe pushed a trio of seventh graders out of the way and struck a *serious* pose in the doorway. She was wearing the most *extra* **Halloween** costume I'd ever seen in my entire life. And *I* was green and about six feet in diameter.

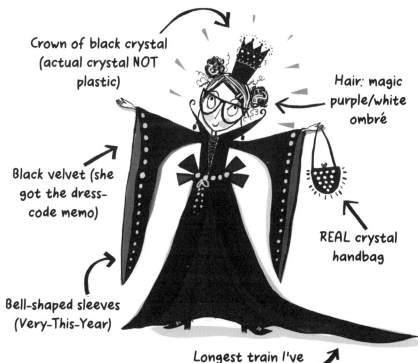

Crown of black crystal (actual crystal NOT plastic)

Hair: magic purple/white ombré

Black velvet (she got the dress-code memo)

REAL crystal handbag

Bell-shaped sleeves (Very-This-Year)

Longest train I've ever seen

She cracked out of her pose at last and sashayed into the middle of the room. "Happy Halloween, witches!" She gave a little twirl. "Now that your queen has arrived, I guess it's time to get this party STARTED!"

"Um, Blair," Fabi snorted. "I think this party has *already* started."

"Yeah," a very cool ninth grader joined in. "It started when Frog Girl arrived!"

Everyone turned to look at me (AGAIN). I gulped. Blair swiveled, very slowly, on her bejeweled heel and faced me.

"Frog Girl?" she spat. "FROG GIRL? *That's* NOT a witch costume and *she* is not even a WITCH, much less a Halloween Queen! What's this?" She flounced over and jabbed at my green belly. "Paper? Green PAPER?!" She swooshed her silk cloak around dramatically. "What sort of **toadbrain** wears—" She broke off suddenly, clasped her hand to her forehead, and a second later the smuggest of smirks spread across her face. "Oh, whatever—it's time for MISCHIEF!" and with that she whipped out her wand and pointed it at ME....

*"With style already wishy-washy,
Make this costume squishy-squashy!"*

But just as she flicked her wand, Puck appeared from nowhere and yelled, "NOT HOPPY!" and rugby-tackled her from behind! They both crashed to the floor. Blair's wand tumbled out of her grip and arched upward through the air, spinning and somersaulting and shooting a chaotic trail of purple sparks toward the ceiling.

Magic on the loose!

There was a rustling, a *rripppp,* and then ... *squealing.* Very nervously, I looked up. *BATS....*

Swooping and diving, so many bats, landing on so many cats and on so many witchy hats. One whole string was down—*a hundred bats!*

My bat decorations were coming to life!

Real ex-bat-decoration bats are
HYPER. Just like Puck had warned.
I'd never seen such an overexcited, giddy,
snickering bunch of flappers in my life.

Oh, no—another string was down! And another!
It was like the runaway magic was leaping from
string to string ... *hundreds* of bats circling the ceiling
in a whirlpool of black wings, sending the Great
Chandelier swinging! They streamed around the
room as disco balls dropped from the ceiling, one of
the serving trees fainted with a great crash, and a
flurry of leaves and students scattered out of their
way, knocking over tables piled high with food as
they went and—

Ughhhh! I had a BAT IN MY HAIR!

Ms. Sparks sprang into action first, pulling out her
wand. "Contain them!" she yelled, looking around
wildly. "Keep them away from the drinks!"

But it was too late—they'd made a beeline
(batline?) for the punch and drained
the bowls in seconds—if they'd been

overexcited before, now on a complete sugar high the bats were out of control! And they weren't the only ones—half of us were yelling and screaming and shaking mini vampires out of our hair and cloaks.

Teachers pushed their way through the panicking crowds, fumbling for their wands. "Don't let them near the cupcakes!" shouted one. Again, too late—a battalion of bats was trailing streamers of colored smoke like the Red Arrows.

"Into the FIREPLACE!" yelled the principal and a herd of obedient witches tumbled toward the grate, sending Zephyr and her golden throne flying. "Not you—the BATS! Steer them into the fireplace and up and out of the chimney!"

Under Ms. Sparks's instruction, all the teachers stopped panicking and swept into the center of the dance floor, flicking their wands and incanting in perfect unison. The tenth graders joined the fray, too, jumping over younger students and pulling cleverly concealed wands from their elaborate costumes. The chanting grew louder and louder until the walls were shaking.

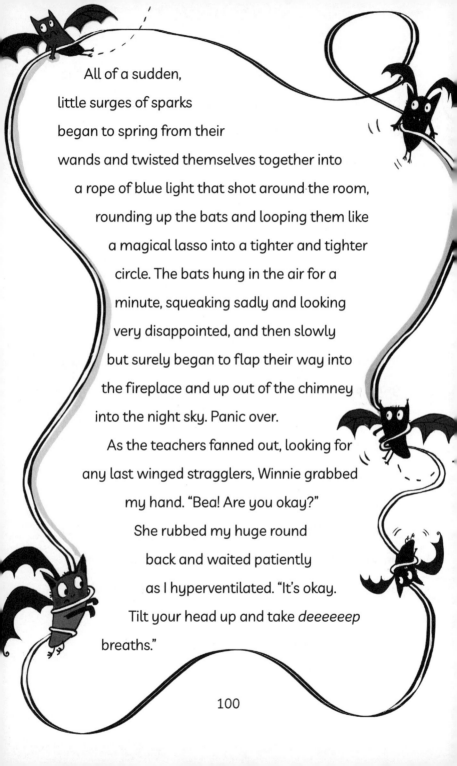

All of a sudden, little surges of sparks began to spring from their wands and twisted themselves together into a rope of blue light that shot around the room, rounding up the bats and looping them like a magical lasso into a tighter and tighter circle. The bats hung in the air for a minute, squeaking sadly and looking very disappointed, and then slowly but surely began to flap their way into the fireplace and up out of the chimney into the night sky. Panic over.

As the teachers fanned out, looking for any last winged stragglers, Winnie grabbed my hand. "Bea! Are you okay?" She rubbed my huge round back and waited patiently as I hyperventilated. "It's okay. Tilt your head up and take *deeeeeep* breaths."

I did as she said and that was when I saw it—*one stray baby bat nibbling through the red silk rope that held up the chandelier!* He was right down to the very last few threads, gnashing as fast as he could, and the whole chandelier was swinging and twisting violently RIGHT ABOVE THE FROG TABLE.

Visions of flying frogs' legs and frogs' arms and all their other froggy parts flashed before my eyes. The chandelier's candles were flickering and starting to go out, spiders were clinging on like it was the *Titanic,* and if it fell witches might get hurt, too!

Before I'd even thought about what I was doing, I had grabbed my wand out of my pouch and pointed it at the chandelier, *willing* it to stay UP. My hand was shaking (or was it the wand quivering?) as another thread snapped and the chandelier jolted. It was coming down! Stan was going to get SQUASHED!

Wishing beyond wishing, I focused as hard as I could and then, by ~~some miracle some magic~~ *my magic,* the chandelier ... STOPPED and just *hung*

there, twirling slower and slower like a big glowing planet in the sky.

Everyone turned to stare up at it. Ms. Sparks looked at me, then at my wand, then back at me. "Great job, Bea!" she gasped, rushing over. "You can relax—we've got it now." Gently, she took the wand out of my hand.

"Was it really *me* that stopped it?" I held my breath.

Ms. Sparks smiled and told me it really, *really* was, that I'd been the only one who'd even seen what was happening. And then she said she'd always known I could do it.

Seriously? *I* hadn't.

"But I'm *ordinary*," I said, and she shrugged in a so-what kind of way. "I'm NOT A WITCH," I tried again.

She laughed and pointed at the chandelier that was even now being rehung on new red ropes as a result of some nifty wand-weaving by Madam Binx and Miss Lupo. "Um, I think you are. How else do you explain what just happened?" I didn't know what to say. "Also, you have a decidedly witchy kinship with frogs." I looked down at Stan, who had hopped onto my big green belly.

"Maybe just this one," I said, and she laughed. "But I'm not from an extraordinary family." I said it again, louder this time—it didn't matter if they all heard because they all already knew. "I'm an *Ordinary*."

"*Pffffff!*" Ms. Sparks flapped her hand like she was swatting away a fly. "Oh, me, too."

Whaaaaaattttt?!

"Nothing to be ashamed of. It doesn't matter where you start, it's where you end up that counts." Zephyr, perched safely on her shoulder again, nodded. "Hard work and belief, that's all it takes—not that that's easy." And then Ms. Sparks told me, loud enough so everyone standing nearby could hear, including Blair, who was looking nervous next to a very angry Mr. Muddy, that she was really PROUD of me.

"It wasn't Blair's fault," I said, suddenly feeling bad. "She was only doing a Queen of Mischief spell."

Ms. Sparks raised an eyebrow and gave Blair a long look. "Halloween mischief should never be directed at one singled-out witch," she said sternly, but before Blair could say anything, Puck spoke up.

"It was MY fault really," he said. "It all went wrong." He looked at me and mumbled, "I'm sorry. I was trying to help."

I grinned at him—I knew that.

"Well," said Ms. Sparks slowly, "it certainly made for a memorable Halloween. *Mistakes,*" she looked from Blair to Puck and back again, "were certainly made, but I don't suppose there's much that can't be fixed with an advanced cleaning-up spell." We all took a moment to look around at the smashed disco balls, upturned chairs, discarded costumes, and squashed cupcakes. "No real harm done—thanks to Bea!"

I turned red again and looked at Winnie and Fabi and Amara and Puck.

"I had help," I said and picked a fat spider out of my hair.

"Didn't someone say something about getting this party started? *Again*." Mr. Muddy was grinning at Ms. Sparks. And on the count of three, they both flicked out their wands, and in less time than it takes me to eat a fluffmallow, everything was the right way up, the punchbowls were refilling themselves, the candles were flaming again, and the disco balls were floating into place.

"DJ Bones on the decks!" shouted Indiana, restarting the music, and with one more swish of Ms. Sparks's wand, little glowing stars strung themselves across the ceiling where the bat decorations had been. "Much safer!" She winked at me, but before I could reply, Fabi and Amara and Winnie and Puck had grabbed me and pulled me onto the packed dance floor.

BEST PARTY EVER.

Afterward, it took me quite a while to get to the car because a) I had to frog-hop and b) I had to say good-bye to everyone because I won't see them until after fall break. Well, except I *will* see Winnie and Puck and Fabi and Amara because we're going to meet at Taffy Tallywick's tomorrow for a major post-party gossip!

"Here," said Winnie as I was about to go. She held out a slightly squished Halloween cupcake. "It was the last one left, and we all thought you deserved it the most."

Oh! I took it carefully and concentrated on the tiny bat-teeth marks in the icing so I wouldn't get TEARY.

"The magic should wear off in about an hour," explained Fabi, "but it will still taste amazing."

I nodded and mumble-thanked them and we all HUGGED (well, as much as we could given my frogginess and without squashing the cupcake any more).

"So?" Dad asked as he rolled me onto the back seat. "Did you have fun?"

I said I'd had **SOOOOOOOOOOOOOO MUCH FUN,** but after a minute of babble about toffee smoke and decorations I *stopped*.... There was so much I was never going to be able to tell him, no matter much I wanted to! But for once Dad wasn't nagging me for details—he couldn't wait to tell *me* something.

"I was going to wait until tomorrow, but maybe this is the right moment."

"What?" I asked, looking at the roof of the car and wishing I could scratch my real tummy.

"It came." He was being very mysterious.

"*What* came?"

"Guess," he said.

I had a head full of Halloween magic and I was *very* uncomfortable and needed to use the bathroom. This was no time for guessing games. "Just *tell* me."

So he blurted it out. "They've accepted you."

"Who?" I asked.

"The **Academy,** of course."

It still took me a minute to figure out what he was talking about.

The **Academy,** with its shiny new buildings and its soccer teams and sensible uniform and sensible everything. Oh. *Oh.*

"B-but," I began as we pulled up outside our house. I was still but-butting when two minutes later in the kitchen he handed me the letter.

Mr. Black
1 Piggoty Lane
Little Spellshire
Spellshire

SPELLSHIRE ACADEMY

Finding the Excellence in the Ordinary

October 30

Dear Mr. Black,

Further to our letter dated October 7, we are now pleased to inform you that we can make a place available to Miss Bea Black as of Monday November 8 (return date from fall break).

Please confirm Miss Black's acceptance in writing.

Yours faithfully,

Dr S. N. Sibbel

Admissions

I *tried* a happy smile.

"You wanted this, right?" Dad was looking at me very closely.

"The thing is," I began. "The thing is...." I scrambled out of my green shell and sat down at the table in my tights and T-shirt. For what I was about to tell him, I really needed to be less FROGGY. "I ... uh ... the thing is ... um...." He was putting me off by staring at me in a very intense Dad-looking-right-inside-me kind of way. "The thing is ... Winnie and Puck and—" I broke off again. I wasn't entirely sure where I was going with this. "Well, Extraordinary, it's not so...," I shrugged.

"You haven't, by any chance, changed your mind about something?"

I nodded.

"Let me guess—you don't want to go to the **Academy** anymore?"

I nodded again, and flakes of green face paint fell onto the table.

"You want to stay at Extraordinary?"

This time I nodded so hard my eyes fell off.*

---

*Not my ACTUAL eyes, my frog eyes.

"Well –" Dad popped a couple of wonky slices of bread in the toaster—"I always say being open to changing your mind is an underrated skill."

He waggled his eyebrows at me and I grinned— that was one of his very favorite things to say. "Good decision, Bea Black," Dad said and burned the toast.

11:44 p.m.

The first thing I did when I came upstairs was open my window and YELL, and seconds later, a sleepy-looking Ash opened *his* window and grinned over at me.

"Good party?" he shouted, and I shouted back that it was absolutely AMAZING and then—because I could hardly give him any witchy details—I lobbed over the leftover Halloween cupcake.

"That. Is. The. *MOST. AMAZINGEST.* Thing. I've. EVER. Tasted!" he yelled through the crumbs, but then his mom came in to tell him to stop shouting and especially to stop insulting her cooking and go back to bed.

I was the only person who noticed the tiniest wisp of green smoke coming out of his nostrils!

~~11:59 p.m.~~ Midnight

I didn't see it until I was getting into bed—a package tied up in brown paper and string tucked under the covers....

Another brand-new DIARY!

Happy Halloween, Bea!
I thought you might be
needing this! Dad xx

There's just enough space left in this one for one last list....

Things I Will ACHIEVE Next Semester Now That I Have Friends

- Master all the trickiest GO skills including the Flying Cat Swerve and the Boggle Dodge.
- Persuade Dad to buy me a puppy (also ask if I can stay on frog rotation because of STAN). 🖤
- Be the best co-captain of the Dodos since the time of Minerva Moon.
- Find out who Minerva Moon ~~is~~ was.
- Learn to cook/make potions/bake.
- Ask Blair to teach me how to do the loop-the-loop on my broom.
- Levitate STUFF!

SIXTH GRADE CLASS PHOTO

READ ON FOR A SNEAK PEEK OF
BEA'S NEXT MAGICAL ADVENTURE!

SECRET SPELLS

MONDAY NOVEMBER 1

11:03 a.m. Home

It's the first day of fall break, I'm still in my pajamas, and I've had three cookies for breakfast and half a packet of fluffmallows that I found under my pillow. What is even more impressive is that I managed to *levitate* the fluffmallows with my WAND all the way from the bed to my mouth.

It feels weird writing in a new diary. The pages are so empty, and there are almost no crossings-outs or mistakes or missed days or lists of things I have NOT managed to do (like potion spells). It's so clean and perf—

11:11 a.m.

The thing about fluffmallows is that they are very STICKY.

I've hidden my old diaries in the back of my sock drawer because it is *very* important that NO ONE ever reads them. Especially not Dad because I never did learn to write in code – **EDOC? FRGH? £0D*?** – and it will only take him about a nanosecond to find out that I'm a ~~witch~~ witch-in-training. That's the kind of shock nobody wants to give a parent.

I feel bad keeping such a big secret from Dad, but it's his own fault for making us move to Little Spellshire and *then* accidentally sending me to the School of Extraordinary Arts instead of the perfectly ordinary **Spellshire Academy**. If it hadn't been for that one tiny classic-Dad-mix-up, I probably still wouldn't even know witches *existed*, much less be learning how to become one.

Witches, when they're not hanging out with other

witches (like at WITCH SCHOOL), are very hush-hush about their witchiness. As our principal, Ms. Sparks, always says, "Those of us who know, *know* and those of them who don't, *can't*."

So, even though Dad's mistake turned out to be the most amazing mistake in the history of mistakes, I can't tell him. If I did, I'd probably have to turn him into a toad* or maybe Ms. Sparks would turn *me* into a toad—or maybe we'd BOTH be turned into toads. (I can't really imagine any of my teachers turning somebody into a toad, but I've learned the hard way that in Little Spellshire, it's best not to rule anything out.)

11:22 a.m.

I *can* imagine some people in my class turning ME into a toad.

Hunter Gunn? Izzi Geronimo?

Definitely Blair Smith-Smythe!

*NO IDEA how to do this.

ABOUT THE AUTHOR*

Bea Black is eleven years old and has recently
moved to Little Spellshire, where she lives with
her dad, a weather scientist. She has no pets,
but has been on class frog rotation this semester.
Her lifelong dream is to get a puppy.
This is Bea's second diary.

*With a little help from Perdita and Honor Cargill!